J. T.

J. T.

by Jane Wagner

With Pictures by Gordon Parks Jr

VAN NOSTRAND REINHOLD COMPANY
NEW YORK   CINCINNATI   TORONTO   LONDON   MELBOURNE

West Harpswell School

TO EVA AND THE FAMILY

Van Nostrand Reinhold Company Regional Offices:
Cincinnati • New York • Chicago • Millbrae • Dallas

Van Nostrand Reinhold Company International Offices:
London • Toronto • Melbourne

Published by Van Nostrand Reinhold Company
a division of Litton Educational Publishing, Inc.
450 West 33rd Street, New York, N.Y. 10001

Published simultaneously in Canada by
Van Nostrand Reinhold Ltd.

Book design by Myron Hall III
Printed by Halliday Lithograph Corporation
Bound by Publishers Book Bindery, Inc.
16 15 14 13 12 11 10 9 8 7 6

Grateful acknowledgment is made to members of the cast of the CBS *Children's Hour* production of *J.T.* who appear in the photographs as characters in this book: Jeannette Du Bois as Rodeen Gamble; Therese Merritt as Mama Melcy; Kevin Hooks as J.T.; Michael Gorrin as Mr. Rosen; Olga Fabian as Mrs. Rosen; Holland Taylor as Mrs. Arnold; Robert Brown as Boomer; David Ayala as Claymore; Helen Martin as Mrs. Hill; Andrew Monzon as Jeffie Michael; and Alma Hubbard as the lady in the grocery store. We also thank the show's Executive Producer, Barbara Schultz; Producer, Jacqueline Babbin; Director, Robert Young; Art Director, Ben Kasazkow; Costume Supervisor, Joseph Aulisi. Their cooperation was especially helpful to Gordon Parks, Jr. as he made the illustrations for the book during the filming of *J.T.*

Special acknowledgments go to Gloria Safier, Eva Stern, and Addison, Goldstein, and Walsh.

For two days the red convertible had been parked near Mr. Rosen's grocery store. J.T. had noticed it on his way to and from school and had wondered who it belonged to, because not many people in his part of town could afford a set of wheels like it.

What really caught J.T.'s eye was a transistor radio in a leatherette case on the dashboard. He thought how great it would be to hold a radio like that to his ear and tune in on music all the time. It was just a few weeks before Christmas. Maybe if he told his mother that what he wanted most was a radio....

For a moment J.T. almost believed his mother might buy him a radio, but he looked down at his corduroy pants that were wearing thin and letting in the cold, and knew better. His mother would get him something practical, like warm pants.

As J.T. got closer to the car, he could see that the side window was open a crack. Almost at the same instant he saw Claymore and Boomer closing in on the car. J.T. knew what they were up to; he had seen them cop things from cars before. Without stopping to think, J.T. ran to the car, pushed open the window, and lifted the radio out by its strap. He turned and ran. He could hear feet hitting the pave-

ment behind him, and he knew Claymore and Boomer were chasing him and the radio. J.T. raced down the block. His heart pounding like a bongo drum, he watched the traffic for a chance to cross the street. Home and safety were on the other side. Seeing a delivery truck rushing toward him, J.T. held his breath and dashed in front of it—straining his body to the far side of the street. He made it—leaving the truck between himself and the boys.

Before the truck could pass him, J.T. had ducked into the doorway of a tenement being torn down. He peeped around the door and saw Boomer and Claymore sulk off down the street. They stopped at the corner and yelled, "You can't hide forever! We'll get you. Just wait!"

J.T. leaned back inside the door and caught

his breath. His heart was still pounding from excitement, and his hand trembled a little as he turned the radio over to examine it. On the bottom were the words *Made in Japan.* Claymore's and Boomer's threat still echoed in his ears. He clicked the switch on and zapped out their angry words with a loud rocking sound that vibrated from the little radio. He felt as though the music was coming from somewhere deep inside himself, and it made him so happy. His heartbeat mixed with the rock-beat until he couldn't tell which was which. He then half ran, half bugalooed home.

That night J.T. took the radio to bed with him. He always wore his hat when he slept because it kept out the draft from the window next to his bed. He tucked the radio up under the flaps of the hat and radioed himself to sleep. It was a comfort to tune in to music and hear his deep-down feelings played back to him. That way he could also tune out on what he didn't want to hear.

"J.T., You get your bones outta that bed now, you hear?"

His mother's voice seemed to come from way off in the distance, from somewhere just outside the dream he was having. J.T. snuggled down under the blankets. He wished he could disappear into his dream and drive off in the red convertible. The top would be down because he would be going some place warmer.

His mother's voice came closer. "I don't know what's harder—gettin' you *in* bed at night or gettin' you *out* of bed in the morning."

Slowly, J.T. came up from the covers. His mother watched him rub the sleep from his eyes. "By the time I get you out of bed," she said, "I'm ready to go back myself."

J.T. shivered into his corduroy pants and went out into the hall where the bathroom was. Mrs. Hill was coming out of the john, and J.T. turned the radio up as loud as it would go, hoping he wouldn't be able to hear whatever

she had to say to him this morning. There were times when he thought she practiced being cranky.

But the volume wasn't loud enough. She got right in front of him and said, "If I was you, J.T. Gamble, I wouldn't put those batteries so close to my head. Your brains is liable to get transistorized, and then what?"

J.T. felt the blood rise in his face. He wanted to talk back to her, but he went into the bathroom instead. It smelled of cough syrup as it always did in the winter after Mrs. Hill had been in. J.T. wondered if having a cold all winter made a person cranky, or if being cranky made the cold hang on. It was too cold in the john to spend much time wondering about anything, let alone Mrs. Hill's health, and J.T. hurried back to the kitchen.

His mother had lit the oven and all the burners on the stove, and the warmth welcomed him. He sat down at the table and crumbled graham crackers into a bowl and poured milk over them. His mother looked at him.

"I don't want you dawdlin' around after school today, you hear? Mama Melcy's due in at the bus station at four thirty-five sharp, and you got to be there and see her home."

J.T. watched the graham crackers soak up the milk, then spooned in a mouthful.

"Now I'm depending on you. You know she don't take to this city much. She won't know how to get here from the station 'less you be there to help her. You hear me?"

"I hear. I hear." J.T. answered. He pressed his spoon down on the graham crackers, waiting for them to get to the right point of sogginess before taking another bite.

He watched his mother rinsing out her coffee cup. Finally he said, "I could use a little money . . . for the radio. The batteries is gettin' low."

"Those batteries can't get low enough to suit me," she said. "The less I hear from that box the better I like it. Besides, you think I don't know where you got that thing? I'm not contributing nothin' to no stolen object, no

sir! Seems like to me, you such a big-time hustler and all, you might of thought to steal some batteries too."

"Aw, Mama, you all the time naggin' me," J.T. said, wishing he hadn't brought up the subject.

His mother looked at him. "You better be glad you got me to nag you. The law don't nag you. It just tells you. I'm trying to help you before you get in bad with the law, 'cause that's where you're headin', sure as sin, if you don't mend your ways."

J.T. pushed his bowl away from him. He didn't feel hungry anymore. His mother sat down across from him. She looked at him with troubled eyes, and her voice was softer now.

"I don't know what to do no more. Seems like we just growin' more and more apart each day. You're gettin' to be such a disappointment, J.T. Seems like you been turnin' bad since the day your daddy left. If you don't watch out, you're goin' to be headed down the same wrong road he was."

There was a hurtful silence between them, and J.T. did not look at his mother. He got up from the table, picked up his school books and coat, and banged out the door.

Halfway down the stairs he heard his mother call after him. "Four-thirty sharp now, you hear me? You hear me?"

When J.T. reached the street the cold air stung his body. He put on his coat and pulled the hood up over his head. It protected his face from the cold and hid the tears that were streaming down his face from passersby. He could still hear his mother's voice, "Turnin' bad, turnin' bad." J.T. had never felt so alone, except maybe that day when his daddy hadn't come home. He watched the cars groaning and crawling sleepily out of their parking places. He hunched his shoulders against the cold and continued walking.

As he neared Mr. Rosen's grocery, Claymore and Boomer jumped out from a doorway

next to the store. Boomer grabbed hold of him, and Claymore yelled, "We want that radio!"

"Yeah," Boomer snarled. "We saw it first!"

J.T. struggled to free himself. He heard Mr. Rosen shouting, "Hey, what's going on here? What's the trouble?"

For a moment the boys were distracted, and J.T. used that moment to make his escape. He ran past the store and through an empty lot. He could hear Boomer shouting, "Don't worry, we'll get you!"

As he ran J.T. looked over his shoulder to see if they were following. He didn't see the rock ahead of him and he tripped, landing on

his knees and elbows next to a mound of trash. He looked up and saw something looking back at him. He looked closer and saw the scraggy face of an old alley cat. The cat tried to get to his feet, but fell back to the ground.

J.T. pulled some of the trash away from the cat's hiding place to get closer. He could see that the cat had only one eye, but that was from an old battle. It was badly hurt from some recent scrape. His body was a battlefield of cuts, scratches, nicks, and bruises. There was a wide gash at its throat. J.T. saw that the cold air had made the blood clot and stopped the bleeding. That much was good, anyway. The cat tried to get to his feet again, but fell back in pain.

J.T. could hear the school bell urging him to leave. He got up slowly, brushed himself off, and checked the radio in his hat to make certain it was secure, then turned to go.

J.T. reached the edge of the empty lot, then turned and looked back at the cat. He noticed then that the palm of his right hand was bleeding. He wondered what it must be like for the cat to have to stay out in the cold. His scratched hand was stinging now, and he thought that his own pain must be slight compared to the cat's.

"Your assignment is a Christmas composition, "What Christmas Means to Me," Mrs. Arnold announced to the class. J.T. looked around the room. From the expressions on their faces he could tell that some of the other guys thought it was a dumb thing to write about too.

"Your composition is due in two weeks," Mrs. Arnold continued. "You should be able to find plenty of inspiration all around you. Why, even the weather is cooperating. . . ." Mrs. Arnold walked over to one of the windows to look closer at the large snow flakes that had begun to fall. Some of the children had decorated the windows with soap drawings. She stopped in front of one drawing, and

J.T. sat at a table by a window. He hadn't been able to pay much attention to Mrs. Arnold all morning. He cupped a hand over one eye and looked down at his bologna sandwich, then out at the snow. He decided that snow was no less with one eye than with two, and suddenly knew what he must do. He put his sandwich back into the wax paper bag and stuffed it into his pocket. On his way out of the cafeteria he noticed that someone had only half finished his milk. He grabbed the carton and took it with him.

J.T. thought he saw her almost laugh. She turned to the class and said, "All right, who's the Rembrandt in the class?" She was pointing to the drawing of the Three Wisemen. They were all three pretty stringy and the first two were riding the usual camels. The third was riding a motorcycle.

Before anyone could say anything the bell ending class rang. "Class dismissed. No horseplay on the lunch lines," Mrs. Arnold said.

When J.T. got back to the lot, the cat was not where he had last seen him. J.T. looked all around for a place where a cat could hide. He was just about to give up when he thought about the house being torn down at the edge of the lot. He had hidden there many times; maybe a cat would seek shelter there too.

J.T. scrambled up over the broken boards and pieces of rock that were where the back door had been. He was standing in a room that was once a kitchen. One whole wall was torn away, and there were huge gaps in the roof. He found the cat hunched back in the oven of an old abandoned stove. He pulled the mashed sandwich from his pocket and poured some milk into an old Dixie cup. At first the cat shrank back, and J.T. thought he was going to jump out the back of the stove. But the smell of food overcame his fear, and he slowly, painfully, crawled forward and began to nibble at the food.

It was snowing harder now, and the wind was blowing. The cat shivered convulsively each time an icy blast swept through the house. The stove was too open to offer much protection. J.T. began to rummage around the

lot. He uncovered Venetian blind slats, slabs of masonite, asphalt tiles, pieces of old furniture, and a square of windowpane intact with the wooden frame still secure. A window for the cat's house! J.T. worked with a desperate intensity from some wild blueprint in his mind. He didn't hear the bell that beckoned him back to school for the afternoon.

The house that J.T. built was strangely beautiful. He had fitted the windowpane to the back of the stove, and when the door at the front was closed the cat was protected from the wind. An umbrella kept the snow from falling in from above, but allowed air to circulate. Boards were propped along the sides for further protection. As a finishing touch, J.T. made steps leading up to the entrance.

When he had the house completed, J.T. dried the cat off with the inside of his jacket, careful of the cuts and scratches. He unzipped the hood from his jacket and wrapped it snugly around the cat.

"I'm gon' call you Bones," he said. "You ain't hardly more'n that. I reckon you must have been usin' all the strength you got just to keep breathin', with nothin' left over for lookin' after yourself." He put the milk that was left inside the house next to the cat and closed the door.

For a long time J.T. sat and stared through the window at the thin creature inside the house. It began to get dark outside, and the streetlights came on. Before leaving, J.T. stroked the cat's scraggly fur and pulled the hood up securely around him. He looked back on his way out. Bones was watching him.

When J.T. reached the door to his apartment, he heard voices from inside. He remembered that he was supposed to have met his grandmother at the bus station. He closed the door carefully, hoping not to be heard. His mother and Mama Melcy were talking in the kitchen.

"Now, I don't want you givin' the boy no punishment on my account, understand?" he heard Mama Melcy say. "To tell the truth, I'm right pleased with myself, makin' it up here on my own. The trip from down home was easy as banana pudding, but the trip from the station to up here was somethin' else. When I got off, I asked the driver was he sure this was 125th street, and he made a face over at me and said where did I think I was, and I said, 'Oh, excuse me, I thought we might of landed on the Base of Tranquility by mistake.'" Mama Melcy chuckled warmly as she ended her story. His mother laughed too.

J.T. couldn't remember how long it had been since he'd last heard the sound of his mother's laughter. It stirred long-ago feelings inside him. But the sound quickly turned sour.

"I should have met you myself," his mother said. "I don't know. Lately he's just gone bad. Lyin' and stealin', and I don't know what all else."

Mama Melcy turned and looked through the kitchen door. Seeing J.T. standing there, she smiled down at him and reached out her arms.

"Mmmmmm-mmmmh, if you ain't a sight to see."

J.T. felt himself being swooped up into her arms and swung around and around and around. Then she held him at arm's length and said, looking him over, "Can't say that you've growed none though. You just as string-beany as ever. J.T. threw his arms around her and

buried his head in her soft shoulder. From across the room, he could feel his mother's eyes staring at him.

Mama Melcy, sensing the tension between them, said, "Well, let's eat now. I'm hungry as a berry picker."

J.T. sat down at the table at his grandmother's suggestion. His mother brought the turnip greens and cornbread to the table, and sat down stiffly. J.T. watched as Mama Melcy broke up her cornbread into her glass of buttermilk and then took her spoon and started to eat. J.T. took some turnip greens onto his plate and stared down at the green potlikker running out of them. He didn't dare look at his mother.

Mama Melcy looked back and forth at her daughter and grandson, wishing there were something she could do to bring them closer together.

"These instant products is right good, Ro-deen," she said. "Ain't much use startin' from scratch anymore. I sure am hungry. When I got off the bus, I felt faintlike from not eatin'. So I come upon one of them food machines..."

Sensing that her story was warming them up, she continued, "I was ready to try anything, so I reach into my pocketbook and get out a quarter and push it into that place where it says to, and then I punch grape soda—and do you know what that contraption did? Oh, it spurts out grape soda all right—only it forgets the paper cup."

J.T. could not keep from laughing now, and his mother joined in.

"I'll say one thing though," Mama Melcy continued, "I got my quarter back. Leastways that contraption was honest. *Dumb,* but honest."

Rodeen got up from the table and started to clear the dishes. "Even a machine knows you can't get by with being dishonest," she said.

J.T.'s grin faded. He looked down at his plate. He wondered if the cat would like turnip greens. He doubted it. He felt Mama Melcy's eyes on him and looked up. He liked the way Mama Melcy was looking at him. He thought if he ever took a trip in that red con-vertible, maybe he'd stop by for a visit with her down home.

Mama Melcy leaned closer to J.T. and asked, "What you want for Christmas, child?" J.T. looked at her for a long time.

"A cat," he said. Then, gathering his determination, he continued. "I want me this cat I found. You reckon I could have him? Could I? He needs a home. He's real bad off, near dead, almost. Could I?"

A long silence followed.

His mother got up from the table and scrapped the leftovers from her plate into the garbage can, then said, "I don't have me enough troubles, I got to nurse me a half-dead cat. Anyhow, only animals they allow in this place is rats."

"But Mama, he's liable to die. Please... couldn't I keep him? I'm afraid he'll die." J.T. looked anxiously from his mother to his grandmother.

"Well," his mother replied, "a cat's got nine lives. Losin' one won't matter much."

J.T. went into the front room and switched on the television. He had just finished supper, but somehow he felt empty inside.

Later that evening as he was getting ready for bed, Mama Melcy was unpacking her old cardboard suitcase. When she finished, she crossed over to the window. "You sure got some peculiar windows in this house, openin' out onto solid brick walls. Maybe that wall is a machine, and if you put a quarter in and punch 'view' you'd get . . ."

"With my luck, you'd get grape soda," Rodeen replied.

Mama Melcy laughed and said, "With or without the paper cup?"

It was good having Mama Melcy around, J.T. thought. That night J.T. lay in his bed with the tiny radio next to his ear. The room was dark except for the lights from across the street that visited J.T. every night.

Popping in uninvited, flexing their neon muscles . . . Bar and Grill . . . Bar/Grill/Bar/Grill . . . throbbing in and out of the room, pulsating electronic messages across J.T.'s body and over the walls. J.T. stared blankly at the lights, unable to sleep.

He wished he could send his own messages out through the night to the house where Bones was. He wondered if Bones felt as alone as he did. He closed his eyes, but sleep was nowhere inside him. He had too many feelings and worries in his head, and there was just no room for rest.

He got out of bed, dressed and slipped quietly out the door. Maybe, he thought, the radio would make the cat feel less lonely. It had helped him, maybe it would do the same for Bones.

J.T. made his way through the night streets. He was a little scared of his neighborhood at night. He didn't like to admit it, but he was. There were two men on the corner drinking something wrapped in a paper bag. They had lit a fire in a trash can and were huddled over it trying to keep warm. J.T. thought they looked lonely too.

When he reached the house, he walked as silently as he could. He didn't want to waken the cat if he was asleep. He looked in and saw Bones staring up at him. His one eye was lit up like a light—as though he had a flashlight battery inside his head for nighttime use.

J.T. put the radio inside the stove next to the cat's ear, adjusting the volume and station to what he thought would be to Bones' liking. The batteries were fading out, so he turned the radio vertically and then horizontally for the best reception.

He checked the wounds and petted the cat gently. J.T. felt a warm vibration that made him smile. He had never felt a cat purr before.

Bones blinked up at J.T. sleepily. J.T. pulled the hood up closer around the cat's shoulders and turned to leave. He looked back several times before disappearing into the night. If it had not been so dark, he would have seen Bones watching out the window of his beautiful home, staring after his new-found friend for as long as his one eye could focus clearly.

The next morning J.T. was half way out the door when his mother called to him. "Wait, J.T., you got to go to the store before school." She handed him a grocery list. "Here, charge it," she said. "If he says anything about the bill, tell him I'll get straight with him soon as I get paid. Now run on."

J.T. looked up at Mr. Rosen, then down at his list. "A pound of lard, a quart of butter-milk, and a half dozen eggs, please," he said.

As Mr. Rosen gathered the items, J.T. looked carefully through the cluttered rows of canned goods. His eyes seemed to be mag-netically drawn to the tuna fish section. Bones would like tuna fish, he thought. As Mr. Rosen handed him the bag of groceries, J.T. looked up at him, then over at Mrs. Rosen, then down at the list. He was staring so hard at the list that he thought his eyes might burn a hole through the paper. Pretending to read from the list, he cleared his throat and said, "Oh yes, four cans of tuna fish too." As Mr. Rosen put the tuna into the bag, J.T. added, "Charge it, please. My Mama say she'll give you what she owes you as soon as she gets paid."

As he turned to leave, Mrs. Rosen called after him, "Tell your mother it's been two months now and not a penny." J.T. looked back at her, worried that she might take the tuna fish away. As he went out the door, he heard Mr. Rosen say to his wife, "Sarah, don't, not to the boy. What are you worried? We're so starved we can't give a little credit?"

Mrs. Rosen answered back, "Giving people a break is one thing, Abe. Letting people take advantage of you, that's another. Face it, Abe, you got a heart like a sponge cake. You treat this store like it was a Care Package. You're the original Mr. American Express Card, himself."

J.T. hurried back home with the groceries.

and git yourself to school," she said, with a laugh. Mama Melcy always made him feel good. He dodged her playfully and skittered out the door.

On his way he had taken the cans of tuna out of the bag and stuffed them into his pockets. His mother and Mama Melcy were in the kitchen having coffee. He walked passed them and put the bag on the kitchen counter. Then, making sure no one saw him, he took the can opener from the kitchen drawer. Mama Melcy grabbed him as he was leaving and jokingly spanked him on his behind. "You better scat on outta here, Mr. Fiesty Pants,

A few minutes later, J.T. was where he most wanted to be—beside the cat. He checked on the wounds first. They seemed better, but Bones drew away in pain when J.T. went near the gash in his throat. J.T. opened a can of tuna and offered him small pieces with his fingers.

J.T. fed him more and more until the can was empty. Bones looked up at J.T. as if to say thank you, and licked a flake of tuna from his whiskers. Then, meticulously, he began to clean himself. J.T. was delighted with the sudden show of strength. In the distance he heard the school bell. It was time to leave.

On his way to class, J.T. saw Boomer and Claymore coming down the hall toward him. Trying to avoid them, he quickly ducked into the restroom. The two boys ran after him.

J.T., backed up against the wall, begged them to leave him alone. At the sight of his fear the two bullies became bolder. Boomer shoved J.T. and snarled, "Come on. Come on and hand it over! Where's the radio?"

"I don't have it. Honest." J.T. answered.

When the boys realized that J.T. really didn't have the radio, they got meaner. They shoved him up against the sink and pushed his head down into it face up under the fau-

cet. There was a plastic container of liquid soap directly above J.T. Claymore pushed the knob and the harsh germicidal soap dripped down into J.T.'s eyes.

J.T. felt as though the inside of his head was on fire. He struggled to get free, but Boomer had a strangle hold on him, and Claymore kept punching the soap container. J.T. tried to scream, but Boomer clamped his hand tightly over his mouth to muffle his cries. Only when they heard the outer door swing open, did they relax their hold on him. They ran out, almost knocking over Jeffie Michael as he came in. J.T. turned the water on his face, trying to wash the stinging soap out of his eyes.

"What's the matter with you?" Jeffie asked, seeing J.T. hung over the sink with water splashing over his head.

J.T. rubbed his eyes. "My eyes," he said. "I . . . can't see."

Jeffie held his glasses up to the light to clean them. "Maybe you need glasses, like me," he said, matter-of-factly. He reached across for a paper towel to dry his glasses, then turned to J.T. "Say, you know that motorcycle? Under the Wiseman? You know who drew it?"

J.T. looked up at Jeffie, water and tears still streaming down his face. "Was it you?" he asked, trying to put out of his mind what had just happened to him.

Jeffie grinned down at J.T. "Yep, it was me." They smiled at each other. J.T. was glad to be let in on the secret.

"Boy, you sure can draw good," he said, looking up out of his bleary eyes, definitely impressed. "Can you draw cats?"

"Oh, sure, I could if I wanted to. Only I don't want to. I just like to draw motorcycles. I got seventy-three drawings of motorcycles. All of 'em are on paper except the one in Mrs. Arnold's room. That's the only one I got on glass."

"When they wash the windows, it'll be gone," J.T. said.

They both felt sad for a moment, then Jeffie changed the subject. "Hey, your eyes really look bad. I'm sure you need glasses. Listen, don't worry if you do. They're not so bad. You get used to them." He turned to go and bumped smack into the corner wall. He grinned back at J.T. "You have to be careful not to break them though." He went jauntily out the door, leaving J.T. with his head still hanging over the sink.

J.T. spent that night making an eyepatch for Bones. With great care and concentration, he cut up an old Halloween mask. He squinted down at his work, his own eyes still burning from the soap. He felt as though he knew now more than ever how the cat must feel being partially blind. He hoped Bones hadn't had a similar experience to his when he had lost his eye. Just thinking about his run in with Boomer and Claymore made J.T. shiver. As he cut and pasted, he heard his mother and Mama Melcy talking from the front room.

"He's up to somethin', that boy." Mama Melcy chuckled.

"He always is," his mother said. "He don't have his radio on though. That's peculiar. I get so used to that thing blarin' all the time, I get bothered by it being off now as much as on. Wonder how come it's off tonight?"

"Maybe the batteries is dead," suggested Mama Melcy.

"Could be," his mother said, nodding. "Could be."

Mr. Rosen had barely opened up the gates to the store when J.T. came bounding in the next morning. "Three cans of tuna fish, please, and some masking tape," he said.

Mr. Rosen frowned down at him, then reluctantly put the items into a bag and handed it to J.T. "Uh . . . , charge it, please," J.T. said, his eyes fastened to the edge of the counter.

Mr. Rosen, not exactly happy with the transaction, got out his ledger and wrote down the amount.

As J.T. started to leave, Mr. Rosen headed back to his meat compartment for the day's supply of meat. Mrs. Rosen stopped him, making him put on his muffler and hat.

"How many times do I have to tell you?" she nagged. "You'll turn into a frozen Birds-eye vegetable. There. *Ge gesundtei heit.*"

"It's not Alaska I'm going to, Sarah. It's my meat compartment," Mr. Rosen grumbled.

J.T., glad Mrs. Rosen's attention was on her husband and not him, left the store quickly. He tiptoed up to the little house. He peered in through the window and smiled when he saw a wide eye peering back at him. The eye looked as though it had been awake for hours.

J.T. put the eyepatch around the cat's bad eye and secured it by taping it down with masking tape. Bones blinked up at J.T. as if in disbelief. He seemed to know he looked great in an eyepatch. J.T. held up the bottom of a tuna can so Bones could see himself.

J.T. thought he looked positively heroic, and he was sure Bones shared his opinion.

They looked back and forth at each other. In honor of the occasion Bones ate a heroic breakfast that morning.

J.T. had brought iodine and Band-aids from the medicine chest at home, and after Bones had finished the tuna he looked over all the wounds and painted those not healed with iodine.

He tried to put a Band-aid over the open

cut at his neck, but Bones cried out in pain and scratched J.T. on the hand. J.T. decided to put the Band-aid on himself instead.

He petted the cat to reassure him that he understood he hadn't meant to hurt him. Bones purred loudly under the stroking.

Suddenly J.T.'s hand went rigid. His palms began to perspire, even though it was cold.

He could see Boomer and Claymore heading toward the house. He held his breath until he saw them cross the street and turn into another block, apparently unaware of J.T. and the cat. J.T. thought they hadn't seen him, but he couldn't be sure.

Rodeen Gamble discovered that J.T. had been charging things to her grocery account a week later when she went to pay her bill. Mr. Rosen gave her an itemized list of purchases, which she studied carefully. She looked at Mr. Rosen, puzzled by what she saw.

"Look to me like there's been some mixup. I never bought no tuna fish . . . ," she said.

"Mrs. Gamble," Mr. Rosen reasoned, "would I cheat you? Believe me, your son. He's been coming in a lot lately—buying tuna fish as if it was going out of style."

Rodeen looked at Mr. and Mrs. Rosen, distressed. "That sums up to be more than I expected," she said.

"The little boy with the radio in his hat—he's yours, isn't he?" asked Mrs. Rosen. Rodeen nodded. "Then there's no mistake," Mrs. Rosen said firmly.

Rodeen shook her head. "Ever' time I get a dime's worth of difference between me and my bills, that boy does something to set me back." She got out her money and counted it carefully. "From now on, please, don't sell him nothin' on credit 'less you see it down on paper as my list."

"Listen, don't worry," Mr. Rosen said.

Mrs. Rosen spoke up, "That's right, Mrs. Gamble, don't worry. It so happens you're dealing with a very rich man. He's so rich it wouldn't surprise me if the government should knock on that door any day now, asking *him* for Federal aid."

Rodeen felt uncomfortable, and left the store quickly. That same morning, J.T. sat by the cat's house. He was making a welcome mat for the grand mansion. Every day, he had made something new for the house. Today it was the welcome mat. He considered the spelling of the word WELCOME for some time, then printed it as carefully as he could on the tile. When he finished it, he put it in front of the house for Bones to see. It was obvious that the cat liked it.

Bones stopped purring when he heard the school bell ring. It usually meant that J.T. was about to leave. But J.T. did not leave. He hadn't left yesterday or the day before either, preferring to stay with the cat all day, playing builder and architect. The house was quite magnificent now—with a shabby kind of elegance about it, much like Bones himself.

When the welcome mat was finished J.T. played veterinarian. He had found a scrap of rubber hose which he used as a stethoscope

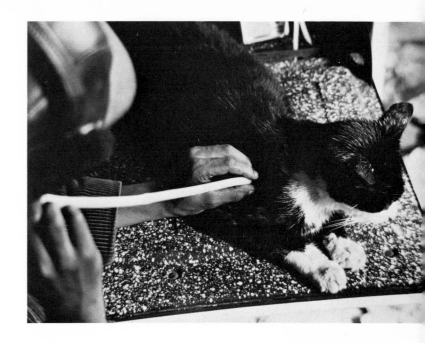

to listen to the cat's heart. He took the cat's paw in his hand and, looking at an imaginary watch on his wrist, pretended to take the cat's pulse. Then he checked Bones' heart. The cat looked up at J.T. as if to say, "Will I live?"

As Bones' health had improved, so had his appetite. They were out of food. J.T. decided he'd better make a trip to the Rosens' store to stock up on tuna.

As he entered the store, he saw Mr. and Mrs. Rosen exchange glances with each other. He took a deep breath and said, "Two cans of tuna fish, please, and charge it."

"No more credit for you, young man," Mr. Rosen said sternly. You're a very bad boy—

cheating on your mother. You should be ashamed. What are you up to anyway?"

"Your mother works hard for the little she earns," Mrs. Rosen added. "You should be helping her. Instead, you're a heartache. You're on your way to becoming a full-fledged bum. Some *chupspa* you got—some nerve. From now on, the only kind of credit you get in this store is *dis*credit!

J.T. felt his heart turn over. He backed away, hurt and ashamed and frightened. He looked back and forth at them for a moment, his back against the door. He then turned and ran out.

At the house J.T. went through the used cans of tuna, trying to find something left in them. Bones licked the oil that remained in some of the cans. J.T. felt like crying, but he didn't want Bones to see that he was upset. He fought back the tears and leaned down and whispered in the cat's ear, "Don't worry, I'll get you something."

Bones looked into his eyes as if to say, "I know you will."

J.T. decided to go to school. He could get food at the cafeteria. That was what he was doing when Mrs. Arnold saw him. J.T. closed his eyes and wished she would disappear.

When he opened them again, she was closer than before and coming toward him.

"Well, J.T.," she said, "what made you honor us with a visit today?" J.T. ducked his head. "You know," she continued, "you're not Santa Claus. We expect you to visit us *more* than once a year. Have you finished your composition—What Christmas Means to Me?"

"Not quite," J.T. answered, shifting to one foot, then to the other.

"Then I think you'd better stay after school and work on it. See me in my room this afternoon—I'll be there grading papers." Mrs. Arnold turned to leave, then looked back.

"None of which will be yours, I might add. Be there."

That afternoon J.T. sat fidgiting at his desk trying to concentrate on the assignment. His mind kept floating away to the empty lot. Mrs. Arnold's voice seemed far off as she spoke to him.

"It's too bad we don't have a course in

missing persons, J.T. You might pass that. I'm not sure you'll pass anything else. You know that when you fail, you fail more than just a grade in school. You fail yourself as well."

She got up from her desk and went over to him. "How much have you done?" she asked, looking down at his notebook.

J.T. lowered his head and squirmed around in his seat. "Please, could I go now? I got something real important I got to do . . ."

Mrs. Arnold was exasperated at not being able to reach him, but felt he was deeply agitated about something. "I'm disappointed in you, J.T. I expected more. Oh, all right, you're not doing anything here anyway. Go on."

J.T. jumped up and dashed out through the cloakroom. As he shut his notebook, a paper fell out and fluttered to the floor. Mrs. Arnold bent down to pick it up. She looked at it carefully. At the top of the paper, he had written:

What Christmas Means to Me

by J.T. Gamble

Christmas means . . .

The writing trailed off and underneath he had made a squiggly little drawing of the cat

he cared for so dearly. Mrs. Arnold started to crumple it up and throw it away, but something stopped her. She didn't know exactly what it was, but something made her want to keep the paper. She smoothed it out, opened her desk drawer, and put it inside.

As J.T. rounded the corner toward the empty lot, he sensed something was wrong. He ran to the little house and looked anxiously inside. Bones was gone.

Suddenly Boomer and Claymore jumped him from behind, yelling and leaping toward him Karate-style. J.T. felt the blood leave his face when he saw Claymore swinging the cat

back and forth. Boomer had the radio and waved it at J.T., threatening to drop it. They circled him again and again, taunting him—first with the cat, then with the radio.

J.T. lunged back and forth between the two, trying frantically to get to Bones, horrified at what they might do to him. He could hear the cat crying out for help, struggling desperately to get away.

Boomer tossed the radio to Claymore. It

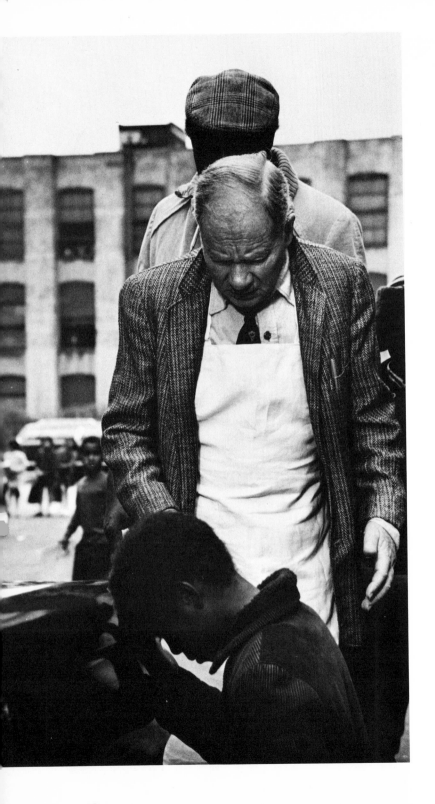

went over J.T.'s head and Claymore caught it with one hand while he held onto the cat with the other. He threw it back to Boomer, skillfully avoiding J.T.'s outstretched hands. But when Boomer tried to return it again, his throw was high—far out of Claymore's reach. The three boys watched as the radio sailed through Mr. Rosen's window with a loud crash. Then the two boys started to run. Claymore dropped the cat, and Bones, terrified, darted out into the street.

Panic-stricken, Bones zig-zagged into the path of a car. The car swerved wildly as the driver tried to miss the cat. Bones screamed out at the moment of impact.

J.T. ran into the street. He wanted to run after the car, but the driver hadn't stopped. All J.T. could see was an orange day-glow bumper sticker disappearing down the block.

J.T. made himself look down. Bones lay at the curb. His sides heaved, and there was a trickle of blood at his mouth. J.T. picked up the cat's broken body and carried him over to the little house. He could feel that life was gone as he put him inside.

Mr. and Mrs. Rosen had seen the accident. Mr. Rosen went to J.T. and put his arm around him. "Son," he said softly.

J.T. kicked him away and huddled against the house, sobbing uncontrollably. Mr. Rosen stood back watching him helplessly, not knowing what to do. He understood about the tuna now.

Mrs. Rosen saw Mama Melcy walking toward the store, on her way to do Rodeen's shopping. She met her midway and explained about the accident. Mama Melcy dropped her shopping cart and ran to J.T.'s side.

"Honey," she said, reaching out to take him in her arms. J.T. looked up at her, tears frozen on his face. Then he ran off across the lot.

Mama Melcy looked after him, then down at the strange construction beside her. Bending over, she looked inside and saw the cat's lifeless form. She recognized the hood from J.T.'s coat. She took it and slowly put it in her pocket. Mr. and Mrs. Rosen came up behind her.

For a long moment, they stared at the little house. Mama Melcy saw something at the entrance and picked it up for a closer look.

49

It was the welcome mat. She closed her eyes and shook her head slowly.

"I knowed his heart was in a tangle 'bout somethin'," she said, "but I didn't know what. He spent one whole evenin' makin' that patch for that poor critter's eye."

Mr. Rosen looked around the empty lot, then back at the little house. He was moved by its valiant attempt to be a home.

"Look . . . out of all this junk . . . just look at what he made."

That night when Rodeen got home from work Mama Melcy told her about what had happened that afternoon. They both tried to comfort him in the days that followed, but J.T. wouldn't be comforted. He only nibbled at his food, though Rodeen fixed things she knew he liked, and he talked little.

"If only I'd listened to him," Rodeen told

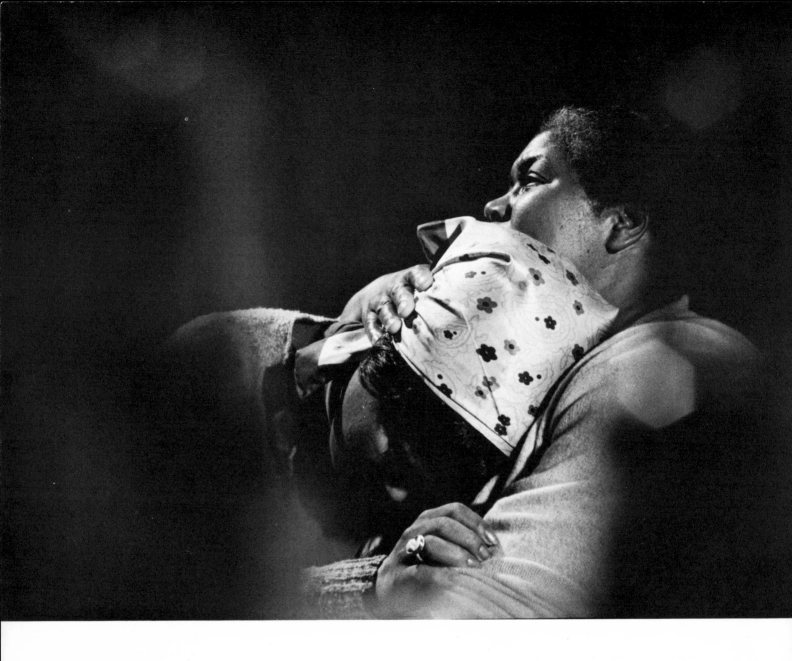

Mama Melcy. "If only I'd let him bring that cat into this house when he asked. . . . If only . . ."

"Yes, if only you had," Mama Melcy told her. "But you didn't, and now we have to listen to him all the more. What's done is done. Ain't no use in you blamin' yourself for what you can't undo." Mama Melcy understood J.T.'s grief, and she knew there was little she could do to lessen it.

One night, late, she went in to talk with him after he had gone to bed. J.T. did not stir when she entered the room, but he felt her presence at the end of the couch. She checked the draft and tightened the cloth stretched across the window.

"I made some boiled custard. How 'bout I get you some?"

J.T. shook his head no.

Mama Melcy sat down on the couch and put his feet in her lap, making sure the blanket was tucked in around them. She was silent for a moment. They both stared at the neon lights that flickered their messages across the walls.

"I don't know why we decoratin' a tree," she said. "This place is lit up like a Christmas tree as it is."

She turned to J.T. and smiled, then rested her head back on the antimacassar pinned to the couch. There was an awkward silence again, then Mama Melcy began to speak— painfully at first, then easier as she sensed that she was reaching him.

". . . I know how bad you hurtin', honey. That cat, he was somethin' real special to you, I know. You . . . you somethin' real special too. You are."

J.T. looked down at the blanket, studying a corner of it intently. Finally he asked, "Why did it have to happen? Why?"

Mama Melcy shook her head slowly. "Why? . . . Oh, child, I wish I could give you the answer, but I can't. Seem like life got a whole lot more questions than answers to it. Seem like they ain't no answers to no question that don't end up, if you wait long enough, bein' jes' another question of a different sort."

J.T. listened carefully, and she continued. "You start out young askin' questions and you end up old askin' questions. And the puzzlement is, they mostly the same questions. They's jes' a few years in between where you think you got answers to match up to the questions."

J.T. thought about what Mama Melcy was saying, then said, "At school . . . when we have tests . . . sometimes I 'bout miss every question there is." Suddenly he felt his pain again, and whirled around, beating his fist on his pillow. "Why did it have to happen. Why?"

Mama Melcy patted him soothingly. "Death is a mean way to have to learn about life. . . . But that's the way of it sometimes. That's just the way of it."

They were silent for a while. Then J.T.

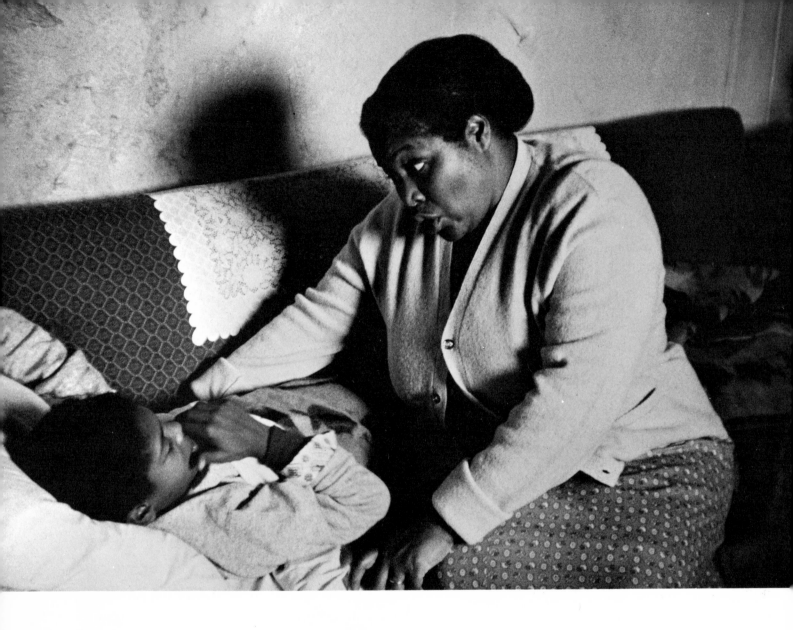

spoke. "What Mama said about a cat havin' nine lives. That's just an old sayin', ain't it? Ain't no truth to it, is there?"

"Well, now. They's some truth to all them old sayin's. That's how they got to be old sayin's . . . 'cause they's partial truth to 'em."

J.T. turned and looked at her hopefully. "Then maybe Bones . . . maybe he's got some lives left. Maybe four or three or . . ."

"Sure he has . . . sure he has," Mama Melcy assured him. "He's jes' gone some place better to live 'em, that's all." She paused for a moment, then looked directly into his eyes and said, "But you . . . what about you? You jes' got *one* life to live. What are you gon' do with it?"

J.T. buried his head in his pillow. "I don't understand," he said. "I just don't understand nothin'."

Mama Melcy tucked the covers up around his shoulders. "What you got to understand, child, is yourself. And that ain't no easy matter, 'cause you are a right complicated little person. You are."

She bent down and put her arms around him, rocking him back and forth for a long moment, gently stroking his head. Then she held him at arms length and looked straight into his eyes again. "If you want answers," she said, "maybe you jes' better listen to your heart."

She smiled and poked him in the chest. "The batteries ain't dead in there." She gave him a big squeeze, kissed him goodnight, and got up to leave. On her way out, she eyed the neon lights flashing on and off across the walls.

"Bar and Grill . . . Bar and Grill . . . Peculiar wall paper . . . peculiar," she muttered to herself. J.T. stared after her.

The next day Mr. Rosen was watching through his window when J.T. passed on his way to the empty lot. J.T. approached the little house with his head down. Then, slowly, he looked at it, trying hard to fight back the tears. He stared a long time at the welcome mat at his feet. He grabbed it suddenly and flung it out across the sky. It landed near the piece of rubber hose he had used to listen to Bones' heart.

He picked up the hose and toyed with it—remembering and thinking. He put one end of the hose to his ear and the other to his chest and listened thoughtfully. Slowly he

rolled it up and stuffed it into his pocket. He looked at the house one more time, then, unable to bear it any longer, turned and ran off down the street.

That night J.T. watched television after supper while his mother and Mama Melcy went to prayer meeting. They had just come home, and Mama Melcy was commenting on how she liked the way the preacher talked, when the doorbell rang.

It was Mr. Rosen, huffing and puffing from climbing the six flights of stairs with his arms full. Mama Melcy and Rodeen looked at each other, startled by Mr. Rosen's unexpected visit.

"Come in. Come right on in," Mama Melcy said warmly.

Mr. Rosen gave her the basket he was carrying and said, "No, no. I can't stay. I just brought this by. It's a little something for the boy."

The something moved in the basket. Mama Melcy looked down into it cautiously. Underneath Mr. Rosen's muffler she saw the wide eyes of a scrawny kitten—as startled as everyone else seemed to be. She set the basket down on the floor and said, "Well, what a surprise. Look here what Mr. Rosen done brought to put under the Christmas tree."

J.T. looked the other way, pretending not to be interested.

"I found him in the street," Mr. Rosen explained. "I thought maybe the boy would take care of him." He looked back and forth at the three of them anxiously. Both Rodeen and Mama Melcy looked at J.T., but he kept his eyes glued to the television set.

Mr. Rosen continued, "It won't cost you a penny. From the store . . . you can have food and everything it needs. No problem."

The kitten struggled to free itself from Mr. Rosen's muffler. It crawled out of the basket, dragging the muffler with it. Then, free at last, it did a Halloween cat dance across the floor. The three grownups laughed.

Rodeen was deeply touched. "We thank you," she said. She got down on the floor next to the kitten and went through the basket, finding the radio among the cans of tuna and the bag of kitty litter. She held it up for J.T. to see. He barely acknowledged recognition.

Mr. Rosen started to leave, and Rodeen stopped him. "Wait, you forgot your muffler."

Mr. Rosen took it from her. "Women!" he grumbled. "You've all got mufflers on your minds. Well, goodnight, goodnight."

Mama Melcy closed the door behind him. "Well, now. Who say there ain't no Santa Claus?" she said. "You jes' never know what's gon' happen. . . . You jes' never know."

The kitten began to explore the room. It sniffed every piece of furniture and examined each corner. It stopped in front of J.T. and rubbed its head on his outstretched foot.

Mama Melcy saw J.T. look at the kitten out of the corner of his eye. She looked at Rodeen. "It's beginnin' to feel a little like Christmas, ain't it?" she said.

Later that night J.T. lay in bed watching the neon sign flicker on and off and listening to music from his radio. He couldn't find any music he liked. He tried all the stations but nothing fitted his feelings. He heard a soft "meow" beside him. He looked down and saw the kitten looking lost and lonely. J.T. turned over on his stomach and reached down and scratched behind its tiny ears. The kitten blinked and began to purr contentedly. J.T. swept the kitten up into bed with him, and they both went to sleep.

The next morning as J.T. came out of his building he stopped dead in his tracks. There was the red convertible, parked almost in front of his house. He stared at it and made a decision. As he bounded up the stairs to his apartment two at a time, the thoughts that had been jumbled in his head for some time began to make sense.

Mama Melcy and Rodeen looked up startled when he bolted through the door over to his bed. He got the radio out from under his pillow and rushed out again. Curious to know what all the commotion was about, they both went to the window and looked out. They saw J.T. emerge below them and go over to the red convertible. He pushed open the side window and put the little radio inside.

Rodeen began to cry. "He gon' be all right. He gon' be all right," she said. Mama Melcy put her arms around her daughter.

J.T. turned away from the car and saw Boomer and Claymore staring at him. Somehow he felt different about them now. He looked straight at them, daring them to start something. Then he walked between them. He did not look back. He knew they would not be following him. He kept going down the block until he reached Mr. Rosen's store.

He went inside and found Mr. Rosen checking the stock behind the counter. They exchanged looks, then J.T. blurted out, "I come to ask you for a job."

Mr. Rosen's expression was thoughtful. "As

a matter of fact," he said, "I could do with some help.

"It's almost a half hour before time for school. Can you start now?"

J.T. nodded.

"Sarah," Mr. Rosen called to his wife. "Sarah, the boy..."

Mrs. Rosen interrupted him. "Abe, we need a rice delivery. Write it down on the list," she said.

"Why?" Mr. Rosen wanted to know. "We still have half a carton full."

Mrs. Rosen came to the front of the store. "You know, Abe. That's the difference between us. To me, the carton is half empty. To you it's half full." She pondered the matter lightly. "I wonder who's right? You or me?"

Mr. Rosen smiled. "I am," he said, and put his arm around J.T.

"Sarah, I've decided. The boy, he's coming to work for us."

Mrs. Rosen squinted at her husband, then at J.T. Mr. Rosen pointed to the meat compartment. "Behind that door, to the right, there's a tray of sausages. You can bring them out, huh?"

J.T. went for the door. He was struggling to open it when Mrs. Rosen called to him.

"Wait," she said, and reached for Mr. Rosen's muffler. "Here, you'll catch your death in there. It's like North and South Pole put together. She wrapped the muffler around him, and smiled at him. Then she pinched him on his cheeks. *"Ge gesundtei heit,"* she said.

J.T. looked at Mr. Rosen for help. "Do I have to wear this? Do I?"

Mr. Rosen smiled broadly, obviously tickled at what he saw. He shrugged his shoulders helplessly and nodded yes.

Mrs. Rosen helped J.T. with the heavy freezer door. Mr. Rosen watched them for a moment, then went over to the door and looked out onto the street.

"It's beginning to feel like Christmas,"J.T. said.